AuthorHouse™ LLC
1663 Liberty Drive
Bloomington, IN 47403
www.authorhouse.com
Phone: 1-800-839-8640

Illustrated by Susan Shorter

Published by AuthorHouse 11/19/2013

ISBN: 978-1-4918-3914-0 (sc)
ISBN: 978-1-4918-3915-7 (e)

Library of Congress Control Number: 2013921208

authorHOUSE®

The Mystery of the CHRISTMAS Thief

by MIKALA PETERS

Illustrated by Susan Shorter

One dark and quiet Christmas Eve long ago, Santa Claus visited We Town. Under the light of a big, bright full moon, Santa landed his sleigh and reindeer on the snow-covered street. He started his long night of deliveries to good little boys and girls. While the children slept behind closed doors, he laid the gifts on the front stoops of houses without fireplaces. He tiptoed up and down the stairs and hallways of the apartment buildings, carefully placing the children's wishes by each of their doors. Whenever he saw a wreath or stocking hanging on a door, Santa hummed a little bit of "Jingle Bells." Recalling from memory what each child wanted, Santa left the hallways and stoops full of dolls, bikes, games, skates, toy cars, and trucks and presents wrapped in red, white, and green paper.

While on the third floor of one apartment building, Santa suddenly stopped in his tracks. His belly felt uneasy. Santa looked over the railing and thought he saw a shadow move in the stairwell. He called out, "Rudolph, is that you?" No one answered. When Santa looked for the shadow again, he saw nothing, so he got back to work. Santa had many more towns to visit. He had to work fast.

A little later, outside one house, Santa felt uneasy again. A cold breeze passed across the back of his neck. He thought he heard the crunch of snow behind him. He quickly turned his head, hoping to see what he heard and felt. But like before, there was nothing. Santa felt much colder. He shivered as the coldness seeped through his red suit and his thick, white long johns. Santa thought out loud, "My imagination must be working overtime." Then he smiled, climbed in his sleigh, and went on with his deliveries.

On that same Christmas Eve, Santa and his reindeer landed on the roofs of houses that had fireplaces. Santa grabbed his overflowing red bag. He scurried down the fireplace chimneys and landed in the homes of snoozing children. Happy to see the Christmas lights and decorations in the houses, Santa hummed as he left the toys and presents for the boys and girls.

Finally, Christmas morning came. Santa had come and gone. In every household in We Town, little boys and girls woke up squealing with excitement. The boys and girls with fireplaces gathered their presents and toys from under their Christmas trees and gleefully opened their gifts. The children that lived in apartments and houses without fireplaces raced to their doors that opened to hallways and front stoops. The children were happy and laughing when they pushed open their doors. Suddenly, the laughing stopped. Their wide eyes searched and searched. The children looked left, and they looked right. The children looked up, and they looked down. Tears filled their eyes and fell down their cheeks because they saw no toys or presents. The gifts had disappeared. Instead, there were puddles of water on the floor and icicles on the doorknobs.

A loud howl vibrated through We Town. It sounded like lots of dogs howling at the moon. The people of We Town rushed to their televisions, radios, and computers to look at the news. Everyone wanted to know what was going on. They learned that the loud howl was the crying and sobbing of the children whose toys and presents had disappeared. Soon after, *all* parents and children put on their coats, hats, and boots to march down to We Town City Hall. Their steps were so many, so loud, and so hard that the whole town shook. We Town's mayor was waiting outside city hall.

Far away at the North Pole, Santa also heard the crying and sobbing of the children. He saw the news about the disappearance in We Town. He immediately ordered his helpers to We Town to search for the missing toys and presents. Santa told his helpers to find a way to make the crying and sobbing children feel better now on Christmas Day. Santa did not want the children to feel sad.

At Christmas time, Santa's helpers were always a part of We Town. They looked somewhat like Santa Claus because they wore red suits, had white beards, and wore red hats. They came in all shapes and sizes: tall and short, thin and wide, light and dark. While Santa was busy making toys and checking to see who was naughty or nice, Santa's helpers walked in We Town Christmas parades, listened to the children's Christmas wishes in the stores and malls, and rang the bells outdoors. As the crowd of parents and children gathered in front of City Hall waiting for the mayor to speak, the helpers walked through the crowd, whispering in the children's ears. They whispered one word: "Share." Before the mayor could say anything, the crowd began to sing, "Share, share because we care for boys and girls everywhere."

The mayor was delighted, and she shouted, "What a great idea!" She proclaimed, "This Christmas Day is also Sharing Day." She asked the parents and children who lived in houses with fireplaces to share their toys and presents. She asked them to share by taking a gift to the school's assembly hall by noon. She then told the parents and children without Christmas toys and presents to go to the school in the afternoon and pick out gifts to take home. The crying and sobbing stopped. Everybody in We Town began to feel better. Both the children that were giving and receiving gifts felt good. All the way home to the houses and apartment buildings, the crowd sang, "Share, share because we care for boys and girls everywhere." Then Santa's helpers got busy looking for the missing toys and presents.

The search started with help from Santa. He told his helpers about the shadow in the stairwell and about his belly feeling uneasy.

"And remember," said one of the helpers, "the children talked about icicles on the doorknobs." Santa then described how he felt a cold breeze on his neck and heard a crunch in the snow at one particular house. The helpers started there to look for clues.

That house looked like a good one to live in. It was made of brown brick with two big white-framed windows in the front. A big white door sat between the two windows. On the door was a Christmas wreath made of candy canes. There was a stoop with two steps that led up to a large welcome mat. Santa's helpers looked on the stoop, beside the stoop, and around the stoop. They found broken icicles. They walked to the left side of the house, looked around, and found nothing. They then went to the right side of the house and stopped in their tracks. Down in the snow, Santa's helpers saw very big prints. They bent down low to the snow-covered ground to look closely at the prints. They looked like big footprints, but not look like Santa's boot prints. One set of footprints went to the house, and another set of the footprints were leaving from the house. Santa's helpers followed the footprints leaving from the house.

After walking a little while, Santa's helpers came upon pieces of red, white, and green wrapping paper. The wind was blowing the pieces of paper across the snow-covered ground. The pieces looked like little red, white, and green dancers moving back and forth, up and down. Santa's helpers became excited, looked at each other, and nodded their heads up and down. When their chins were up in the air, they saw lots of icicles hanging from a tree.

The helpers eagerly started to follow the big footprints in the snow again. They felt they were getting close to finding the missing toys and presents. Suddenly, they came to a stop so quick that they almost tripped over each other. They didn't see footprints anymore. Instead, they saw a gigantic, deep hole in the ground. At first glance, it seemed the footprints just fell into the hole. But the prints had really led Santa's helpers to We Town's salt quarry, the place where the town got the salt that melted the ice from the streets and sidewalks in the winter.

Santa's helpers inched closer to the edge of the hole. They carefully peeked over the edge and saw a footpath that led to a cave inside the quarry. Holding hands and holding their breath, Santa's helpers bravely walked very slowly down the footpath to the cave. Step-by-step, with their backs to the wall, the helpers slowly and quietly made it to the cave. A gray glow lit up the cave, and then they saw the shadow. It looked like it was ten feet tall. The shadow's head looked as big as a beach ball, and its outstretched arms were as long as hockey sticks. The shadow seemed to move like a sail in the wind, and when the shadow moved toward the opening of the cave, Santa's helpers let out a loud gasp.

"Who's there?" the shadow called in a booming voice. It came right to the opening of the cave, then disappeared. As Santa's helpers turned to run, the shadow called to them, "Don't run! You might slip and..." But before the sentence was finished, Santa's helpers were falling into the deep, gigantic hole. Together, as one voice, they yelled, "Santa Claus! Help!" In the blink of an eye, Santa swooped in and caught his helpers in his sleigh.

Once Santa made sure all of them were okay, he noticed crying coming from inside the cave. Santa pulled his sleigh alongside the cave and told his helpers to come with him. The cave looked spooky. Flashlights were lit everywhere, and their beams were flickering, as if the batteries would go out any minute. The areas of the cave that were not lit by the flashlights were almost completely dark. When Santa's helpers touched the cracks in the wall of the cave, some of the wall crumbled and fell. Dust floated in the air.

As Santa and his helpers walked through the cave, they saw piles of toys and presents stacked everywhere. Santa and his helpers had found the missing gifts.

Some of the presents had been opened. Gift boxes and wrapping paper were thrown about the cave. Santa and his helpers followed the trail of empty boxes and torn wrapping paper. They noticed that the deeper they walked into the cave, the colder it got. When they got as far back as they could go, they finally saw the Christmas thief.

A crying figure was huddled in the back of the cave.

"Don't cry," said Santa.

"But they fell into the big hole," sniffed the figure. Each time a tear fell from his eyes, it froze on his face.

In unison, Santa's helpers chimed, "Santa Claus and his reindeer saved us!" The Christmas thief stood up. He looked with surprise at Santa, then at the helpers.

Santa and his helpers also looked surprised. When the Christmas thief stood up, he was so tall that he could dunk a basketball without jumping up. A coat of ice hung from his shoulders. His hair looked like a crown of icicles. When Santa and his helpers looked at the thief's face, they saw what looked like one long, frosted eyebrow across his forehead.

The Christmas thief started to ask Santa, "How did you …?"

Santa interrupted and said, "I just used my magical powers. But now tell me, why did you take these toys and presents from the boys and girls?"

The Christmas thief said, "I saw the toys and presents in the hallways and on the front stoops. They were just sitting outside the apartment and house doors. I'm from Me Town. There, everything is locked away behind closed doors. In Me Town, the people are selfish, so we just take things. We never ask. So I just took the toys and presents."

Santa's helpers exclaimed, "Oh no! How rude!"

Santa asked, "Well, why are you living in a cave in We Town instead of living in Me Town?"

The Christmas thief explained, "I used to have a small house in Me Town. I lived by myself, but I grew so tall that I kept bumping my head on the ceiling. I also got too tall for my clothes. The long sleeves on my shirts came to elbows. My long pants came only to my knees. My feet grew so big that I had to wear clown shoes. I couldn't wear my clothes anymore, and I couldn't live in my house anymore, so I couldn't live in Me Town anymore."

Santa asked, "Couldn't someone in Me Town help you? Did you ask for help?"

"Oh, no!," the Christmas thief exclaimed. "People in Me Town never offer to help, and they never ask for help. In Me Town, you get things, you keep things, and you take things. You don't share."

Santa shook his head and said, "That's so sad. What were you doing with the toys and presents?"

"The toys are all still brand new. I have not played with them," said the Christmas thief. "But I opened some presents. I was looking for something warm to wear. I looked for a warm coat, some long pants, a shirt with long sleeves, and big shoes that fit me. Look at me. Because nothing fits me, I stay very cold. I shiver and shake all of the time. When it rains or snows, the raindrops and snowflakes freeze all over me. You saw my teardrops. They froze on my face."

Santa's helpers said, "Well, just ask for help!"

The Christmas thief softly said, "I don't know how."

Santa said, "Then we will teach you. What does p-l-e-a-s-e spell?"

The Christmas thief thought a little bit, squinted his eyes, and guessed, "Please?"

Santa's helpers clapped their hands.

Santa asked, "What does h-e-l-p spell?"

The Christmas thief said, "Help."

Santa's helpers clapped their hands again.

Santa asked, "What does m-e spell?"

The Christmas thief loudly said, "Me!"

Santa's helpers clapped once again and excitedly said, "Okay, now say those words together."

The Christmas thief took a deep breath and slowly said, "Please help me."

Santa smiled and said, "Of course I will." He went to his sleigh and came back with his big, red, overflowing bag. He dug down deep into the bag and pulled out a warm coat, long pants, a shirt with long sleeves, and shoes that fit big feet. He gave it all to the Christmas thief and said with love in his voice, "Merry Christmas!"

The Christmas thief, with tears in his eyes, said, "I think I know how to use two more words now. Thank you."

Santa said, "You're welcome. Now, quickly put on your new clothes. We have work to do." With a wave of his hand, Santa magically packed all of the toys and unopened presents into his big, red bag. While Santa packed, his helpers went through the cave, turning off the flashlights. Sometimes they would stand in front of the flashlights, laughing at their own spooky shadows. Santa finally said, "Everybody, let's go." Then Santa, his helpers, and the Christmas thief climbed into the sleigh and flew back to We Town. With his new clothing on, the Christmas thief began to warm up. His teardrops thawed, the crown of icicles changed to curly hair, and his one frosted eyebrow became two.

The sleigh bells were so loud that they announced Santa Claus's return visit to We Town. Again, parents and children put on their coats, hats, and boots, then excitedly went to city hall. And as before, the mayor of We Town was waiting outside.

When the sleigh and reindeer landed, Santa and his helpers got out. The mayor walked over and stood next to Santa, who looked out over the many faces and announced to the crowd and said, "We found the missing toys and presents." The crowd cheered, clapped, and stomped so loudly that Mrs. Claus heard them all the way in the North Pole.

"Calm down," Santa said. "Someone else wants to speak." He leaned into the sleigh and whispered, "What's your name?"

The Christmas thief said, "I'm called Chilly Billy." The crowd became so quiet that they could hear each other breathing. Santa said to the crowd, "My helpers and I met our new friend, Chilly Billy, living in the quarry's tallest cave. He wants to tell you what he learned today." Chilly Billy stepped out of the sleigh and stood up straight. The crowd said "*Oh*" and went quiet again.

"I want to say that until today, I did not know how to ask for help. When I saw something I needed, I just took it. That's what we did in Me Town. But Santa and his helpers taught me how to say 'Please help me,' and Santa happily helped me. He gave me warm clothes that fit. I took the toys and presents. But now I want to say something else that is new to me. I'm sorry."

After a pause, a child's small voice broke the silence. It was barely a whisper. "Need help? Just ask. We will help you with the task." Just like earlier in the day, the entire crowd sang, "Need help? Just ask. We will help you with the task."

The mayor of We Town stepped forward and said, "Quiet! Quiet! I have a great idea! Mr. Chilly Billy can live and work at the lighthouse tower. How tall he is will not matter there." The crowd clapped their hands and shouted, "Yes!"

The mayor then said, "This Christmas Day and Sharing Day are twice as nice. Only We Town has been visited by Santa Claus on Christmas Eve and Christmas Day." She asked Santa, "Will you please take all of the found toys and presents to the school's assembly hall where all of We Town's children can take more gifts?"

Santa said, "Of course I will." The crowd clapped and cheered again.

The mayor yelled, "Calm down!" The crowd became quiet again. The mayor said, "Before anyone leaves city hall, I have a present for Santa Claus."

"What?" sputtered a surprised Santa.

The mayor cleared her throat and said, "Santa, for all of your hard work and kindness, We Town presents to you the key to the city." The mayor reached in her pocket and took out a big, long silver key. She handed it to Santa. Another really loud cheer broke out.

Santa put his hand over his heart and said, "Thank you." Then Santa placed the key to the city on his North Pole key ring. Right before the crowd's eyes, the silver key turned into a bright gold key that sparkled like the sun. The crowd again said "*Oh!*" Then Santa told the parents, children, and mayor of We Town, "This key becomes magical in my hands every Christmas Eve. With this key to the city, I can open *all* doors to put toys and presents inside every apartment and home, with and without a fireplace. Thank you, We Town."

He and his helpers stepped back into the sleigh. Santa laughed his big belly laugh, saying, "Ho, ho, ho." And with the snap of his finger, the sleigh was gone.

CPSIA information can be obtained
at www.ICGtesting.com
Printed in the USA
BVHW01s1752071018

529493BV00008BA/446/P